THE TRIAL OF HISSING SID

Written by Jeremy Lloyd
Drawings by Keith Michell

illustrations based on the characters created by
Keith Michell for the Captain Beaky book
published by Chappell Music Ltd.

First published in Great Britain in 1980 by
Chappell Music Ltd., 50 New Bond St., London W1A 2BR
in association with
Elm Tree Books, 57-59 Long Acre, London WC2E 9JZ

*Captain Beaky & His Band — Polydor Album No 2383462
*Captain Beaky & His Band — Polydor Cassette No 3170462
*Written by Jeremy Lloyd, Music by Jim Parker
featuring Jeremy Lloyd, Keith Michell, Harry Secombe,
Peter Sellers, Twiggy
*Captain Beaky & His Band — Keith Michell — Single — POSP 106
*Trial of Hissing Sid — Keith Michell — Single — HISS 1
*Dilys The Dachshund — Penelope Keith — Single — POSP 157
Captain Beaky — Book — Chappell — ISBN 0 903443 38 4
*Captain Beaky — Songbook — Chappell — 2183

Made and Printed in Great Britain

Captain Beaky and his Band were all at Artful Owl's house high in the big hollow oak tree. It was obviously a very special occasion because Reckless Rat's hat and overcoat were very nicely brushed and pressed, Batty Bat had combed his hair, Captain Beaky was wearing his best naval cap with a brightly polished badge and Timid Toad was washing his muddy feet in a small tin basin of water.

'I do wish,' said Artful Owl with a sigh, 'that you'd wash your feet before you come to my home, Toad.'

'I did,' said Timid Toad, 'but they got muddy again on the way.'

Owl sighed and, turning to the mirror propped up against the wall, he gazed at his reflection. 'How do I look?' said Artful Owl.

'That white curly wig and those glasses make you look very stern indeed,' said Captain Beaky.

'And,' said Owl proudly, 'can you see my black legal coat has a beautiful red lining.'

'You really look the part,' said Rat admiringly.

'I am the part,' said Owl. 'I am legal prosecutor at

the trial of Hissing Sid, the evil snake, and you, my friends, are to be witnesses of his evil deeds.'

Bat scratched his head, 'What evil deeds are they, Owl? My memory's very bad.'

Captain Beaky produced a piece of paper, 'I've written them down to remind us,' he said. 'Let me see . . . The stealing of Mandy the Mouse's candy, Abducting a Cuckoo, and Generally Frightening People.'

Toad put his hand up, 'Don't forget he swallowed me. That has to be a crime and it's called, er, now what could that be called?'

'I know,' said Batty Bat. 'Toadacide.'

'That's a good name for it,' said Owl. 'It's quite clear I've got an open and shut case.'

'Oh good,' said Captain Beaky, 'you can put this piece of paper in it.'

'I mean,' said Owl, adopting a pompous legal voice, 'that when I produce the evidence of the evil deeds, the judge will send him to jail.'

Reckless Rat reached into the pocket of his long black overcoat and produced an old watch. 'Time we

were at the Woodland Court. In fact, Owl's spent so long looking at himself in the mirror, we're already late.'

And so, led by Captain Beaky, they ran down the long and winding wooden staircase, out of the front door and into the wood.

In the Woodland courtroom, Lord Chief Justice Pig looked at his big cuckoo clock on the wall and banged his small wooden hammer impatiently on the desk. 'Beaky and his Band are late,' he said. 'I'm not very pleased,' and he gave a loud snort to show how displeased he was.

'They've arrived, sir,' shouted PC Sparrow. 'Come on then, we haven't got all day.'

Captain Beaky, Owl, Rat, Bat and Timid Toad ran up the courtroom steps. They had run so fast that Captain Beaky's best hat had caught in a bramble bush and got torn and the badge was missing, Bat's hair was standing up on end, Rat's best overcoat was covered in leaves and bits of thistledown and fern, and Timid Toad had one very muddy foot because he'd hopped to the court on one leg to try and keep at least one foot clean for the trial.

There was a loud hiss from the Dock and, glancing towards it, they saw Hissing Sid with lots of handcuffs all over him and, on either side of him, all in black, were two Jackdaw jailors.

'I protessst,' hissed Hissing Sid, 'at thisss trial. I am innossscent.'

'Silence in court!' said Lord Justice Pig and, to show how annoyed he was, he shouted 'Silence' again, but the twelve Rabbits in the Jury kept up an excited conversation amongst themselves. Justice Pig banged his hammer twice, 'Order, order, order!' he cried.

Timid Toad put his hand up. 'I'll have a lemon tea,' he said.

'Make mine an ice cream,' said Batty Bat. 'A chocolate one, if you've got it.'

'I mean, silence in Court,' shouted Justice Pig. 'Now, who is defending Hissing Sid?'

'I am,' said the deep rasping voice of QC Crow. 'I am defending this innocent snake from these ridiculous accusations made by Captain Beaky and his silly little band.'

'How would you like a punch in the ear?' said Reckless Rat.

Justice Pig banged his hammer again. 'I won't have talking in my Court,' he snorted. 'The very next person to speak will be thrown out.'

Artful Owl took his wig off and waved it to attract Justice Pig's attention. 'I trust, My Lord,' said Owl, 'as prosecution that I shall be allowed to speak.'

'Yes, yes, of course,' said Justice Pig. 'Now get on with it. What evil deeds has the prisoner done?'

Artful Owl turned to Captain Beaky, 'Captain Beaky, pass me that piece of paper with the evil deeds on will you?'

Captain Beaky took off his hat and peered inside. 'I think it's gone,' he said. 'Oh no, I remember now, I gave it to Rat.'

Reckless Rat put his hand in his pocket, 'Oh yes,' said Rat. 'Yes, it's in here somewhere,' and he searched for a moment, and then he started to look anxious.

'Come on,' said Owl impatiently, 'there must be something in there.'

'There is,' said Rat. 'A large hole. I keep meaning to get it mended.'

'Try the other pocket,' whispered Captain Beaky. 'And be quick.'

Reckless Rat tried the other pocket and gave a smile of relief. 'Here we are,' he said, and handed Artful Owl a crumpled piece of paper.

'My Lords, Ladies and Gentlemen,' said Owl in his loudest and most pompous voice, 'the crimes which the evil snake has been accused of are written on this paper and they are as follows. They are that he did wilfully,' Owl glanced down at the paper, 'collect washing from the laundry, mend hole in overcoat, buy cheese . . .' He looked up surprised, 'What is this?' he said.

'I'm sorry,' said Rat, 'that's part of my shopping list.'

QC Crow held up his hand, 'I think, My Lord, you will agree there is no case to answer.'

'Just a minute there,' said Reckless Rat, 'it's in here somewhere.' And taking off his hat and overcoat,

assisted by Timid Toad and Captain Beaky and Bat, he searched all the pockets inside and out and the lining and inside his hat, but without success.

Artful Owl took the coat and hat and hung it over the rail of the dock and addressed the judge, 'Despite the fact, Your Lordship,' said Owl, 'that we cannot find the legal document to which I referred, my memory is such that I can tell you the crimes that the accused has committed.'

Captain Beaky tugged at the end of Owl's long black coat, 'I'm afraid we're too late,' he whispered.

'What do you mean?' said Owl.

'Look at the Jury,' said Captain Beaky.

'What's wrong with the Jury?' said Timid Toad. 'Rabbits make very good Jurors provided they've got plenty of lettuce and a carrot or two.'

'There were twelve when we started,' said Captain Beaky, 'and look at them now — they've multiplied, there are at least twenty-three.'

'Twenty-four,' snorted Justice Pig, 'there's one under my chair here.'

'This trial is most unfair,' said QC Crow. 'These new arrivals are far too young to know good from bad. I say that this trial should be stopped here and now and I submit that my client is innocent.' With a sweep of his arm he pointed at the Dock.

But the Dock was empty except for two Jackdaw jailors handcuffed together.

'Good heavens, he's gone,' said Rat. 'He's pinched my best overcoat and my best hat.'

'Good heavens,' said Captain Beaky, 'he's disguised himself.'

Justice Pig lent forward and pointed to the jailors with the hammer, 'Why didn't you jailors call out,' he said, 'and tell us that the villain was escaping?'

'You told us not to talk in Court,' one of them replied.

Lord Justice Pig went red in the face, then purple and then, to stop himself saying anything he shouldn't say in Court, he took off his wig and stuffed it into his mouth.

'Quick, men,' cried Captain Beaky, 'we've got to catch that slippery snake.' And, leading the way, he

ran down the courtroom steps and out into the woodland, followed by the others.

'I'll fly up in the sky,' said Bat, 'and I'll send a signal down in morse code the moment that I spot him.'

'We must search high and low,' said Captain Beaky.

'I agree,' said Owl, 'and not forgetting all points in between.'

After a lot of running to and fro and fro and to and twice two and fro, which of course is four, Captain Beaky and his Band — that is all except for Batty Bat, who was just a black dot against the blue sky — paused not far from the river bank, panting.

'It's no good,' said Owl, 'we'll just have to hope that Bat can spot him.'

'I'm not running another step,' said Timid Toad. 'In fact, I'm going to hold my breath and hide behind a tree until he's caught.'

And before anyone could disagree with Toad's plan, he sat down in the shade of a big tree, and took a very large deep breath and swelled up to nearly twice his

normal size and changed colour to match the green of the surrounding grass.

A series of ear-piercing squeaks like a piece of chalk on a blackboard reached their ears, and looking up they saw Batty Bat hovering high above them. He started squeaking in morse code.

'What does he say?' said Captain Beaky.

'SOS,' said Owl. 'I'm afraid it means Snake Out Of Sight.'

Captain Beaky took off his hat and fanned himself, 'Phew,' he said. 'It's getting very warm. Look, how about going for a sail in my biscuit tin, the *HMS Most Leaky*?'

Artful Owl nodded, 'A good idea,' he said, 'this wig's making my head itch.' And, taking off his legal wig, he put it in his pocket.

'Hang on,' said Rat, 'what about my hat and my coat?'

'Who needs a hat and coat in this weather?' said Owl. 'Now, if you really want to wear a coat, you can have mine,' and, taking off his long legal coat, he handed it over to Reckless Rat.

'That's most kind of you,' said Rat. 'It's really quite the best present I've ever had.'

'It's not a present,' said Owl, 'it's just too hot for me to wear it. I shall want it back as soon as we get home.'

And so they went down to the river and boarded Captain Beaky's biscuit tin. Hoisting the handkerchief sail, they got a long stick and pushed themselves away from the bank and out on to the river. It was only then, and Rat was first to notice it, that although Timid Toad had come with them, he was still nearly twice his usual size and his eyes were nearly popping out of his head.

'Look at Toad,' said Rat, 'he's still holding his breath.'

'Oh dear,' said Captain Beaky, 'he's held it so long, he can't let it out. Oh, what are we going to do?'

Artful Owl reached down into the boat and produced, from a great assortment of bits and pieces that were always in the bottom, a large pepper pot. 'This should do the trick,' he said, 'apart from which, the wind has dropped and we need the extra breeze.'

Taking Toad by the arm, he made him stand behind the ship's sail and, holding the pepper pot about Toad's head, he shook it. Toad gave the loudest sneeze anyone had ever heard and he kept on sneezing and the sail pulled the *HMS Most Leaky* along faster than it had ever been before. The sheer joy of sailing on such a lovely day made them all forget about the stuffy old courtroom and Hissing Sid.

But, from a dark hole in the river bank, two beady eyes beneath the brim of Rat's hat watched them as they disappeared round a bend in the river, and from that dark cool hiding place came a long sigh of relief.